For the LOVE of Bubbles

by **Steven Banks**
illustrated by The Artifact Group

Simon Spotlight/Nickelodeon

New York　　London　　Toronto　　Sydney

Based on the TV series *SpongeBob SquarePants*®
created by Stephen Hillenburg as seen on Nickelodeon®

SIMON SPOTLIGHT
An imprint of Simon & Schuster Children's Publishing Division
1230 Avenue of the Americas, New York, New York 10020

Manufactured in the United States of America

6 8 10 9 7 5

ISBN-13: 978-1-4169-1633-8
ISBN-10: 1-4169-1633-4

Library of Congress Catalog Card Number 2005938318

0811 RR2

chapter one

HONK! HONK! HONK! HONK!

It was five o'clock in the morning and SpongeBob's foghorn alarm clock was blaring loudly. He had set it extra early on purpose.

SpongeBob sprung out of bed.

"Good morning, Gary!" he said to his pet snail. "It's another beautiful day in Bikini Bottom and I want to get some bubble blowing in before I go to the greatest job in the world, frying up Krabby Patties at the Krusty Krab!"

"Meow," said Gary.

SpongeBob laughed. "Oh, Gary, you always say that!"

SpongeBob put on his Krusty Krab uniform and went outside with his bubbles and his bubble-blowing wand. He dipped the wand into the bottle, pulled it out, and blew a giant bubble. It looked exactly like a Krabby Patty!

"Wow!" cried SpongeBob. "This is the greatest bubble I've ever blown! I've gotta show Patrick!"

SpongeBob ran over to his best friend

Patrick's rock. "Patrick! Patrick!" shouted SpongeBob as he knocked on Patrick's rock.

"Who's there?" asked Patrick.

"SpongeBob!" said SpongeBob.

"SpongeBob 'who'?" asked Patrick.

"SpongeBob SquarePants!" said SpongeBob.

Patrick laughed. "That's a funny joke!"

"Patrick, it's not a joke. It's my name!" said SpongeBob. "Come out and see this bubble!"

"But I'm asleep!" said Patrick.

"Patrick, how can you be asleep if you're talking to me?" asked SpongeBob.

"Maybe I'm dreaming," said Patrick.

"You're not dreaming, Patrick. I'm real!" said SpongeBob. "Now, come out here! This bubble looks like a giant Krabby Patty!"

Suddenly a gust of wind blew the bubble away.

"Oh, no!" shouted SpongeBob, chasing after his bubble. "It's blowing away! If I let it

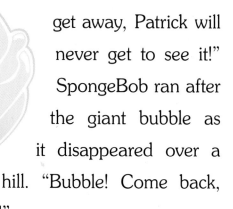

get away, Patrick will never get to see it!" SpongeBob ran after the giant bubble as it disappeared over a hill. "Bubble! Come back, bubble!"

Just then Patrick finally came out of his rock. He looked around, but SpongeBob and the bubble were gone. "I knew I was dreaming!"

SpongeBob was still chasing the bubble. "Bubble, stop! You have to go back and let my friend Patrick see you!" As he passed Shady Shoals Retirement Home, he accidentally dropped his bubble-blowing wand. But SpongeBob didn't stop to pick it up.

He chased the bubble all the way to Jellyfish Fields. While trying to grab the bubble, SpongeBob accidentally dropped his bottle of bubbles. He kept chasing it until he was miles away from Bikini Bottom.

BAM!

Suddenly, SpongeBob found himself facedown on the ground, tangled in kelp. A large bump protruded from his head. He sat up and stared at the sky. "Look at all the pretty stars," remarked a droopy SpongeBob. "They just keep going around and around and arou—"

KERPLUNK!

Just then SpongeBob fell over, and everything went dark. He had knocked himself out!

chapter two

Back in Bikini Bottom, Mr. Krabs was getting mad. SpongeBob always came to work, but today he was nowhere to be seen! "Squidward!" shouted Mr. Krabs. "Where is SpongeBob?"

Squidward was sitting at the cash register, daydreaming about clarinets. "I don't know, Mr. Krabs, but isn't it nice and quiet without him here? I'm almost enjoying my job."

"We're gonna be open soon!" said Mr. Krabs. "If SpongeBob doesn't show up to work, who's gonna make my Krabby Patties? And if no one makes Krabby Patties, then we can't sell any! And if we can't sell Krabby Patties, then I don't make money! And if I don't make money . . . I can't even think about it!"

Squidward jumped up excitedly. "He's gone? Did he move far, far away? Has the day I've been waiting for finally arrived?"

"Who's gonna make my Patties?" bellowed Mr. Krabs. "I'M DOOMED!"

Just then Sandy Cheeks came into the Krusty Krab. "Howdy! Where's SpongeBob? I got two tickets to the new karate movie *Four Fingers of Fear!*"

"He's not here!" said Mr. Krabs. "We've gotta form a search party!"

"Or we could form a celebration party instead," suggested Squidward.

Mr. Krabs took charge. "I'll stay here at

the Krusty Krab, in case he comes back! Squidward, put up posters with SpongeBob's picture on them all over Bikini Bottom! Sandy, go see if Patrick knows anything!"

"That'll be the day!" said Squidward.

Sandy raced off to Patrick's house. "I'll find that little yeller critter!"

Squidward put up posters all over Bikini Bottom. They read, IF YOU HAVE SEEN THIS SPONGE, SEND HIM TO THE KRUSTY KRAB IMMEDIATELY AND TELL HIM TO START MAKING KRABBY PATTIES!

chapter three

SpongeBob opened his eyes. He found himself lying flat on his back, looking up at the sky, tangled in kelp. The top of his head hurt. He reached up and felt a big, sore bump. "Ouch!" he cried. He stood up and was a little dizzy. "I must have bumped my head really hard!"

He saw his Krusty Krab hat and picked it up. "This is a funny-looking hat. I wonder who it belongs to. Maybe I should try to find out who lost it. Or maybe I should leave it here in case someone comes back to find it." He decided to leave it.

SpongeBob looked around. "It sure is pretty out here . . . hey! Wait a minute! Where am I? How did I get out here?"

He sat down next to a pool of water and looked down at his reflection. "Is that what I look like?" He looked closer at his image in the water. "Gee, I'm a pretty handsome fellow!"

Then he looked down at his clothes. "Why am I wearing these pants?

And this white shirt? And a red tie? Hmm."
SpongeBob thought for a second. "Well, I don't
know why I'm wearing them, but at least I know
how to dress!"

In the distance SpongeBob could see what
looked like a big city. "Maybe someone in that
city can help me."

SpongeBob started walking and said to
himself, "That's funny. I can't remember my
name." He kept trying to think of what his
name was, but he had no idea.

When SpongeBob got close to the city he
saw a big sign that said WELCOME TO NEW KELP
CITY! POPULATION: 1,656,076.

Someone is bound to know me here. They'll
tell me who I am, thought SpongeBob.

The streets of New Kelp City were crowded
with cars and buses and taxis. The sidewalks
were jammed.

SpongeBob ran up to a tall man washing a window. He tapped him on the shoulder. "Excuse me, sir. Do you know what my name is?"

"No," said the window washer. "What is it?"

SpongeBob was embarrassed. "Uh . . . I forgot it. That's why I was asking you."

"Well, how am I supposed to know?" said the window washer. "Why don't you look at your driver's license?"

SpongeBob smiled. "That's a great idea!" He reached in his pocket and pulled out a wallet. He opened it up, but there was no license. SpongeBob had never passed his driver's test. "Hmm," SpongeBob said. "I guess I don't have a driver's license." Then he pulled out a note that read, I OWE YOU ONE PIECE OF BUBBLE GUM. It was signed PATRICK STAR.

"Who's Patrick Star?" wondered SpongeBob.

chapter four

Back in Bikini Bottom, Sandy raced over to Patrick's house and found him snoozing. "Pssst! Wake up," said Sandy. "Have you seen SpongeBob?"

Patrick slowly opened one eye. "Uh, no. Of course, I haven't been looking for him either," he said.

"I think SpongeBob's disappeared!" said Sandy.

"Was he in a magic show?" asked Patrick.

"No, he's just plain gone! He didn't show up for work at the Krusty Krab!" exclaimed Sandy.

Patrick's eyes welled up and he started to cry. "Oh, no! SpongeBob's gone!"

Sandy patted Patrick on the back. "Don't worry, we'll find him."

"But where is he?" asked Patrick through his tears. "He might be in trouble!"

"That's why you and I are gonna go find him!" said Sandy.

Patrick jumped up. "I'm on it!" He lifted up his rock and looked under it. "Uh . . . what are we looking for?"

Sandy sighed. "Oh, come on! We are looking for SpongeBob!"

Patrick raised his hand and declared, "I vow that I shall not eat or sleep or go to the bathroom until we find my best friend, SpongeBob!"

chapter five

Meanwhile, SpongeBob was running up to everyone he saw in New Kelp City and asking them if they knew who he was. He also asked people if they knew a Patrick Star.

Nobody did.

SpongeBob finally climbed on top of a statue in the middle of a park and shouted, "DOES ANYBODY KNOW WHO I AM?"

No one answered.

SpongeBob climbed down off the statue.

He sat on a bench and started to cry.

An old man with a cane walked by. "What's the matter, young fella?"

SpongeBob wiped away a tear. "I can't remember who I am, and nobody here seems to know me."

"Well then, maybe you better think of a new name," said the old man.

"But I don't know what my name should be," said SpongeBob.

The old man peered at SpongeBob and scratched his chin. "Well, you're a sponge and you're wearing brown pants and you remind me of a guy I went to school with whose name was Joe. So let's call you SpongeJoe BrownPants!"

SpongeBob lit up. "Perfect!"

Patties! I bet he can still do it! And maybe that'll bring back his memory!"

Mr. Krabs took SpongeBob to the kitchen, handed him a spatula, and put a patty on the grill. It started to sizzle. SpongeBob sniffed. "Mmm. That smells good." Then he began to make a perfect Krabby Patty! Just like he had done a million times before!

"Now do you remember who you are?" asked Sandy.

SpongeBob shook his head. "I do remember

making lots of things into this shape in New Kelp City. But I still can't remember who I am."

"Who cares if he can't remember who he is!" yelled Mr. Krabs. "He made a Krabby Patty!"

"He's gotta remember who he is, too!" said Sandy.

"Can I have a bite of that Krabby Patty, please?" asked SpongeBob. "I'm pretty hungry."

SpongeBob took a bite of the Krabby Patty. "This is tasty!" He took another bite. "This is really good!" He took another bite. "This is delicious. . . . This is . . . THE MOST AMAZING THING I HAVE EVER PUT IN MY MOUTH!"

"Of course it is!" cried Mr. Krabs. "It's a Krabby Patty!"

"Wait!" SpongeBob cried. "It's coming back to me! I work at the Krusty Krab making Krabby Patties! I live in Bikini Bottom, in a pineapple under the sea with my pet snail, Gary! And my name is SpongeBob BrownPants!"

"Close enough," said Mr. Krabs.

SpongeBob laughed. "I was kidding! I know my real name: SpongeBob SquarePants!"

Everyone cheered!

"It's another Krabby Patty miracle!" cried Mr. Krabs. "Maybe I should raise my prices."

SpongeBob put his arms around Sandy and Patrick. "Thanks for coming to find me."

Sandy smiled. "Aw, heck! It was nothin'!"

"That's what friends are for!" said Patrick. "Now let's eat!"

SpongeBob made Krabby Patties for everyone and they had a big party.

"Hey, Patrick," said SpongeBob. "I wish you could have seen the bubble I blew this morning."

Patrick pointed outside the window. "Did it look like that big bubble shaped like a gigantic Krabby Patty that's floating outside?"

They all looked outside and there was SpongeBob's big bubble!

"That's my bubble!" cried SpongeBob.

Everyone agreed SpongeBob's Krabby Patty bubble was the best bubble they had ever seen.

And they were all glad SpongeBob was back home.

Even Squidward.

chapter six

Back home, Sandy and Patrick looked for SpongeBob in all the places that he liked to go to in Bikini Bottom. They made a long list.

"He's gotta be somewhere in town," said Sandy.

First they went to Mrs. Puff's Driving School, where SpongeBob had been trying to get his driver's license *forever*! They found his teacher, Mrs. Puff, at her desk, happily humming to herself.

"Hello, Mrs. Puff. Was SpongeBob SquarePants here today?" asked Patrick.

"No, he wasn't!" said Mrs. Puff cheerily. "No wild car boat rides through Bikini Bottom! No crashes! No smashes! No pain! It's been a lovely day!"

"If ya see him, will you tell him we're looking for him?" asked Sandy.

Mrs. Puff nodded. "Oh dear, I hope you find him. Good luck!"

chapter seven

Meanwhile, back in New Kelp City, SpongeBob still couldn't remember much.

He walked around the city for hours, but no one knew who he was and he didn't see any job that looked familiar to him. SpongeBob rubbed his stomach. He was getting hungry. "I need a job quick, so I can earn money and buy some food!"

He went into a bank that had a help wanted sign hanging in the window.

"Welcome to the Bank of New Kelp City," said a serious-looking little man with a moustache. "I'm the manager."

"Hello, sir," said SpongeBob. "I need a job."

The manager smiled. "Let's give you a try! What's your name?"

"BrownPants is the name," said SpongeBob. "SpongeJoe BrownPants."

He took SpongeBob behind the counter. A customer was cashing a check for one hundred dollars.

"Give the customer her money, Mr. BrownPants," said the bank manager.

SpongeBob took the money out of a drawer. Then he started to flip the money up in the air, just like he was making a Krabby Patty back at the Krusty Krab! Then he folded the money into the shape of a Krabby Patty and handed it to the customer.

"There you go!" said SpongeBob. "One
hundred delicious dollars!

The bank manager yelled, "What in the
world are you doing?"

"Uh . . . I don't know," said SpongeBob. "It
just felt kind of natural to do it that way."

"Well, that's not
the way we handle

money around here!" said the bank manager, fuming. "You're fired!"

SpongeBob tried working at a car factory, but he kept making all the cars into the shape of Krabby Patties. He tried being a construction worker who built houses, but they all ended up looking like Krabby Patties. He even tried being a tailor, but he made a dress that looked like a Krabby Patty!

"Who am I?" wailed SpongeBob. "And why do I keep making things into this strange, tasty-looking shape?"

chapter eight

After the driving school, Sandy and Patrick went to the Bikini Bottom Bubble Blowing Supply Store, where SpongeBob bought all his bubble-blowing equipment. The owner of the store, Mr. Muckle, was behind the counter. Sandy asked him if he had seen SpongeBob today.

He scratched his head. "No, missy, can't say that I have. He was in about two weeks ago. He bought his usual order: two cases of extra bubbly bubbles. He's the only one that buys that kind."

27

Patrick leaned over the counter. "So, in other words, you have not seen SpongeBob today?"

"That's what I just said," Mr. Muckle sighed.

Patrick nodded. "So, what you're saying is SpongeBob is not here!"

"Correct," said Mr. Muckle.

Best Customer

"And you don't know where he is!" said Patrick.

Mr. Muckle rolled his eyes. Patrick folded his arms and declared, "This man is guilty of not knowing where SpongeBob is! I rest my case, your honor!"

Sandy dragged Patrick out of the store. "Come on, Patrick. He isn't here! Let's go!"

When they got outside, Patrick started to feel sad. "Sandy, do you think we're ever gonna find SpongeBob?"

"Course we are!" said Sandy. "Now, don't fret, Patrick. I'm not giving up! No way! No how! I'm not stoppin' till I find that little yeller feller!"

chapter nine

Back in New Kelp City, SpongeBob lumbered down the street feeling sad and lonely. He had tried fifty different jobs and couldn't do any of them right.

Just then he saw a young boy hurrying down the street. The boy's eyes darted around to make sure no one was watching, and then he ducked into an alley. SpongeBob peered down the alley and saw him pull out a bottle of bubbles.

"Hi! What are you doing?" asked SpongeBob.

The boy was frightened. "I-I-I'm blowing bubbles! But don't tell anybody! Please!"

"Why?" SpongeBob asked.

"Blowing bubbles is against the law in New Kelp City. You can go to jail for it!" said the boy.

"That's silly!" said SpongeBob. "Bubbles are fun. They don't hurt anyone. Can I try?"

SpongeBob blew a beautiful bubble.

"That bubble was awesome!" said the boy.

"Thanks," said SpongeBob. "Why is there a law against blowing bubbles?"

The boy explained. "About a hundred years ago, someone blew a big bubble that ended up popping right next to the mayor's ear during a big speech. The loud noise scared him, and he screamed really loudly and then started to cry. He was so embarrassed that he passed a law saying bubble blowing was illegal, and ever since then, it has been!"

SpongeBob frowned. "Somebody should change that law!"

"You'd have to be the mayor to change it," said the young fish.

"That's it!" cried SpongeBob. "That will be my job! I'll run for mayor and bring back bubble blowing!"

"But the election is today!" cried the boy.

"Then I better start running!" said SpongeBob.

chapter ten

Next, Sandy and Patrick went to Shady Shoals Retirement Home, where SpongeBob's favorite superheroes, Mermaidman and Barnacleboy, lived. Patrick burst through the front door. "If anyone knows where SpongeBob is, it's Mermaidman!"

Mermaidman was fast asleep in a chair snoring and Barnacleboy was watching TV.

"Mermaidman? Barnacleboy?" asked Patrick. "Have you seen SpongeBob?"

Mermaidman suddenly
woke up. "Is it dinnertime?"

"Uh, no," said Sandy. "We were
wonderin' if y'all have seen SpongeBob?"

"What's a SpongeBob?" asked Mermaidman.

"He's your greatest fan!" said Patrick.

Barnacleboy looked up from his TV. "You
mean that little yellow square kid that always
comes around and bothers us?"

"That's him," said Sandy.

Barnacleboy shook his head. "Nope. Haven't seen him!"

"Never mind," said Sandy as she and Patrick walked out.

They left the retirement home and started walking down the street. On their way, Patrick looked down and saw something familiar. "Sandy! Look! Here's SpongeBob's bubble-blowing wand! No self-respecting bubble blower would ever leave his bubble wand unattended!"

Sandy gave Patrick a big hug.

"Good job, Patrick. We're on his trail!"

chapter eleven

SpongeBob ran all over New Kelp City putting up big posters with his picture on them. On each poster it said SPONGEJOE FOR MAYOR! HE'LL BRING BACK THE BUBBLES!

Then he went to the park where the election was taking place. Thousands of New Kelp City citizens crowded in to hear his speech

SpongeBob stood at a microphone. "Friends! New Kelpians! Countrymen! My name is SpongeJoe BrownPants and I want to

be your mayor! If I am elected, I pledge to bring back bubble blowing!"

The crowd gasped. "But that's against the law!" they murmured.

SpongeBob solemnly nodded. "The law must change! Bubble blowing has been unfairly banned in New Kelp City! To think that your children cannot enjoy the beauty of bubble blowing, and all because long ago, an innocent bubble happened to pop in the wrong place at the wrong time!"

SpongeBob wiped away a tear. "To think that because of this, children have to sneak around and go to illegal bubble-blowing clubs makes my heart sad! What is wrong with bubble blowing? I say, nothing! I say, bring back bubble blowing! For the young and the old! The rich and the poor! The green and purple and gray and yellow! I have only lived in your fair city for a few short hours, that I can remember, but I already think of it as my home! And I wouldn't want to live in a home where I couldn't blow bubbles! 'What can I, as one person, do to make a difference?' you may be asking yourself. And to that very question I answer: Vote for me, SpongeJoe BrownPants!"

The crowd cheered and applauded. Then

they picked up SpongeBob and carried him on their shoulders through the town, chanting, "SpongeJoe for mayor! Bring back the bubbles!"

chapter twelve

Sandy and Patrick were still on the hunt for SpongeBob. They had just arrived at Jellyfish Fields.

"Next to the kitchen at the Krusty Krab, this is SpongeBob's favorite place to be in the whole wide world!" said Sandy.

"SpongeBob!" yelled Patrick. "Are you out here?" All he saw were thousands of jellyfish. "Maybe he's playing a game and he disguised himself as a jellyfish," said Patrick.

"I'll start asking if any of them is SpongeBob!"
Patrick went up to a big jellyfish. "Hello. Are you SpongeBob SquarePants disguised as a jellyfish?"

The jellyfish stung Patrick.

"Ouch!" he yelled. "If you're SpongeBob, I'm gonna be pretty mad at you!"

Suddenly Sandy yelled to Patrick. "Hey, Patrick! I found something!" She held up SpongeBob's bottle of extra bubbly bubbles. "Yee-haw! SpongeBob was in this here territory."

Patrick took the bubble bottle and put it to his ear and listened. "Yes. He was here many moons ago."

Sandy sighed. "Patrick, he only disappeared this morning! Come on, we're getting close!"

chapter thirteen

Back at the Krusty Krab, Mr. Krabs had brought his daughter, Pearl, to make Krabby Patties.

"But, Daddy!" complained Pearl. "I don't know how to make Krabby Patties!"

"If that little sponge can make 'em, so can you, my precious daughter!" said Mr. Krabs. "And best of all, I don't have to pay you!"

Pearl tried to make one, but it didn't look like a Krabby Patty at all. Mr. Krabs handed it to a customer and he took a bite.

"YUCK! That's the most disgusting thing I've ever tasted in my life!" yelled the customer.

Mr. Krabs's jaw dropped. "It couldn't be as bad as Chumbalaya from Plankton's Chum Bucket."

"It's worse!" said the customer. "I want my money back!"

"The five most evil words in the English language!" shuddered Mr. Krabs. "We must find SpongeBob immediately!" Mr. Krabs grabbed Squidward and shoved him out the door. "Squidward, get out there and don't come back till you find him!"

"But this isn't in my job description!" said Squidward.

"It is now!" said Mr. Krabs.

chapter fourteen

Sandy and Patrick approached the spot where SpongeBob had gotten tangled in kelp and hit his head on a rock. Patrick spotted SpongeBob's hat and picked it up. "Look! Someone who works at the Krusty Krab was out here and lost his hat!" He scratched his chin. "I wonder who that could be."

"It was SpongeBob!" said Sandy.

"How do you know?" asked Patrick.

She took the hat and looked inside. There

was writing inside. It read, THIS HAT BELONGS TO SPONGEBOB SQUAREPANTS. PLEASE RETURN TO THE KRUSTY KRAB.

"Do you think the hat is a clue?" asked Patrick.

Sandy smiled. "Of course it's a clue! We're getting closer to SpongeBob with every step! I can feel it in my bones!"

"I wish I had bones," said Patrick.

Sandy and Patrick started walking toward New Kelp City. As they got closer, they saw the posters

SpongeBob had put up with his picture on them.

"Look! There's SpongeBob!" cried Patrick. "He must be famous!"

"Wait a minute," said Sandy. "It says 'BrownPants for Mayor.' That doesn't make a lick of sense!"

Patrick scratched his head. "Curiouser and curiouser!"

"Let's go find out what's going on!" said Sandy.

chapter fifteen

When Sandy and Patrick arrived at New Kelp City, SpongeBob had just been elected mayor! The citizens of New Kelp City had missed blowing bubbles so much that SpongeBob had gotten all the votes. Dressed up and sporting a black top hat, SpongeBob delivered his victory speech on the steps of City Hall. "As mayor of New Kelp City, I now proclaim that bubble blowing is legal!"

The crowd cheered. SpongeBob handed

out hundreds of bubble wands and bottles of bubbles. Everyone started blowing bubbles!

Sandy and Patrick ran up to the podium.

"SpongeBob, what are you doing here?" asked Sandy.

SpongeBob looked down at Sandy. "Wow! There's something you don't see everyday! A squirrel in a space suit!"

Patrick gave SpongeBob a big hug. "I'm so glad we found you!"

SpongeBob said, "Uh, thanks for the hug, sir."

"No need to be formal," said Patrick. "The name's Patrick, but you can call me Mr. Star."

"Nice to meet you, Mr. Star," said SpongeBob. "Wait a minute. . . . I think you owe me a piece of bubble gum," SpongeBob said, taking the IOU out of his pocket.

Patrick took the note. "How about I give you this hat instead?"

Sandy was still staring at SpongeBob. "Did you go loco, SpongeBob?"

"No," said SpongeBob. "And my name is actually SpongeJoe BrownPants. What's your name?"

Sandy shook her head in disbelief. "You know my name! It's Sandy Cheeks!"

"Well, Ms. Cheeks," said SpongeBob, "I hope you don't mind me asking some personal questions, but what is a squirrel doing in the ocean? And where did you get that funny accent?"

Sandy was getting frustrated. "You know I'm from Texas! Now listen up! Your name is SpongeBob SquarePants! You work at the Krusty Krab! Patrick and I are your best friends, and we're taking you home right now!" Sandy grabbed SpongeBob and his top hat came off.

She looked up and saw the bump on his head. "Hey! Wait a minute! Did you bump your head?"

SpongeBob gently touched the bump. "Yes, I did."

Sandy's eyes went wide. "Now I get it! You must've knocked your head so hard, you got amnesia and lost your memory!"

Patrick jumped up and down. "Let's go find his memory! I bet it's at an ice-cream store!"

Sandy shook her head. "No, Patrick, you can't find SpongeBob's memory. We gotta make him remember who he is."

"I can make him remember," said Patrick. He pointed at himself. "Me Patrick." Then he pointed at SpongeBob. "You SpongeBob!"

"Sorry," said SpongeBob. "I can't remember."

"Well, we're gonna fix that!" said Sandy. "We're gonna take you back to Bikini Bottom!"

"What's a Bikini Bottom?" asked SpongeBob.

"That's where you live!" said Sandy as she started to drag SpongeBob away.

"Hey! You can't take away our mayor!" a man cried, running up to stop them.

SpongeBob turned to the man. "But this squirrel seems to think she knows who I am."

The man began to cry. "But we want you to stay and be our mayor!"

SpongeBob shrugged. "To be honest, all I wanted to do was make bubble blowing legal. Why don't you be mayor?"

The man beamed. "Really? I've wanted to be mayor since I was a little boy!"

"I declare you mayor!" pronounced SpongeBob, and he put his top hat on the man's head.

"Thanks!" said the new mayor.

"Good-bye, New Kelp City!" shouted SpongeBob as Sandy and Patrick dragged him away.

The crowd waved good-bye.

"Thanks for bringing bubble blowing back to New Kelp City!" shouted the new mayor. "We shall erect a statue in your honor! And we shall never forget you, SpongeJoe BrownPants!"

chapter sixteen

Sandy and Patrick brought SpongeBob back to his house. "Do you recognize this place? You live here," Sandy said.

"I live in a pineapple?" asked SpongeBob.

Sandy decided to take SpongeBob inside his house.

"I love the way this place is decorated!" he exclaimed.

"That's 'cause *you* decorated it!" said Sandy.

Gary came out from the kitchen. "Meow."

"Who is that cute little snail?" asked SpongeBob.

"That's Gary," said Sandy.

"Oh, I wish I remembered all of this, but I don't!" said SpongeBob.

"Hmm," said Sandy. "I guess we'll have to really jar his memory."

SpongeBob pointed at Squidward's house. "Who lives in the house that looks like a big face?"

"Maybe SpongeBob will recognize Squidward!" said Sandy. She and Patrick dragged SpongeBob over to Squidward's house.

Squidward was soaking in his bathtub, relaxing from a long day of looking for SpongeBob. Suddenly Patrick ran into the room carrying SpongeBob. "Hey, Squidward! Look, we found SpongeBob!"

Then Sandy came in. "SpongeBob doesn't know who he is."

SpongeBob looked at Squidward. "Sorry, I don't recognize the octopus in the bath tub. But I like his bathroom!"

"Thank you," said Squidward. "I'm glad you like my bathroom. Now will you all please . . . GET OUT OF IT!"

chapter seventeen

Sandy and Patrick decided to take SpongeBob to the Krusty Krab.

"Hey, Mr. Krabs! Look who we found!" shouted Sandy as they ran in.

Mr. Krabs jumped up and hugged SpongeBob. "This is the happiest day of me life! I can make money again selling Krabby Patties!"

"What is this Krabby Patty everyone keeps mentioning?" asked SpongeBob.

Mr. Krabs almost fainted. "In the name of

Neptune, what's wrong with you, lad?"

Sandy explained that SpongeBob didn't remember anything about his former life.

Mr. Krabs started to cry. "But . . . but . . . but if he can't remember who he is, then he might not remember how to make a Krabby Patty . . . NO! It's too horrible to even think about!"

Sandy had an idea. "There's nothin' SpongeBob loves more than making Krabby